Pigeons Don't Growl
and
Bears Don't Coo

PIGEONS DON'T GROWL

AND

Written by
Eth Clifford

Illustrated by
Esther Friend

copyright © 1963 by E. C. Seale & Company, Inc., all rights reserved
Library of Congress Card Catalog No. 63-21736
Printed in the United States of America

BEARS DON'T COO

E. C. Seale & Company, Inc. • Indianapolis

1696964

Mr. Hullabaloo, the angel in charge of sounds, was having a busy day. All the animals had already been given their shapes, but they still had not received their voices. And there he was, with a list of sounds to be given out that was longer than once-upon-a-time spelled backwards, and everybody wanting his sound at the same time. And of course the sounds had to be tested to make sure they were absolutely right! Yes, indeed. It was a very busy day.

"Now, let me see," said Mr. Hullabaloo to himself. "Here we are. Leaves. The leaves will rustle," he read, looking at the list. "My, that's nice. That's very nice."

"Excuse me, Mr. Hullabaloo, sir," said a voice.

"Yes, yes, what is it, Muffer?" Mr. Hullabaloo said to the little cherub who was standing beside him.

"Well, I gave the fire its crackle, and the babble to the brooks, just as you told me to . . ."

"And the patter to the rain?" asked Mr. Hullabaloo.

"Yes, sir. And I've got the wind howling . . . I don't have any more sounds to give out. Are we finished now?"

"Finished? FINISHED? *Buttons and beans!* We've hardly begun! So much to do, and everything to do at once. Here," Mr. Hullabaloo said, tearing off part of the list, "you take care of these animals, and I'll go see about the thunder and the waterfalls. *Walnuts and whiskers!*" he said, hurrying off. "So much to do!"

Muffer looked at the list and sighed. Work. Work. Work. All those roars and moos and quacks and growls to give out before the day's end. When was he ever going to have a little fun?

He put the list down and went to call all the animals together. They were delighted to be getting their voices at last, and so they came as soon as they were called.

"No, no, no," said Muffer, as the animals crowded around him. "No pushing. Everybody in line."

Muffer started to show them how to form a line, and while he was busy, what do you think happened? Donkey, who was a little hungry, and a lot curious, ate the list!

"NO!" shouted Muffer, when he saw what Donkey was doing. *"Now* what am I going to do? I'd better go get Mr. Hullabaloo." The animals looked at him and waited. "No," Muffer told himself. "Mr. Hullabaloo is too busy. I'm sure I can remember who gets what. Nothing wrong with *my* memory."

And so......

Frog got a gobble;
Turkey got a croak;
Dog got a quack;
Duck got a bark;

Cat got a caw;
Crow got a meow;
Cow got a cockle-doodle-doo;
Rooster got a moo;

Bee got a squeal;
Pig got a buzz;
Donkey got a peep, peep;
Chick got a bray!

Lion got a chirp;
Cricket got a roar;
Pigeon got a growl;
Bear got a coo!

"There!" said Muffer, very pleased. "What do you say to *that?* Nobody's been left out. Is everybody satisfied?"

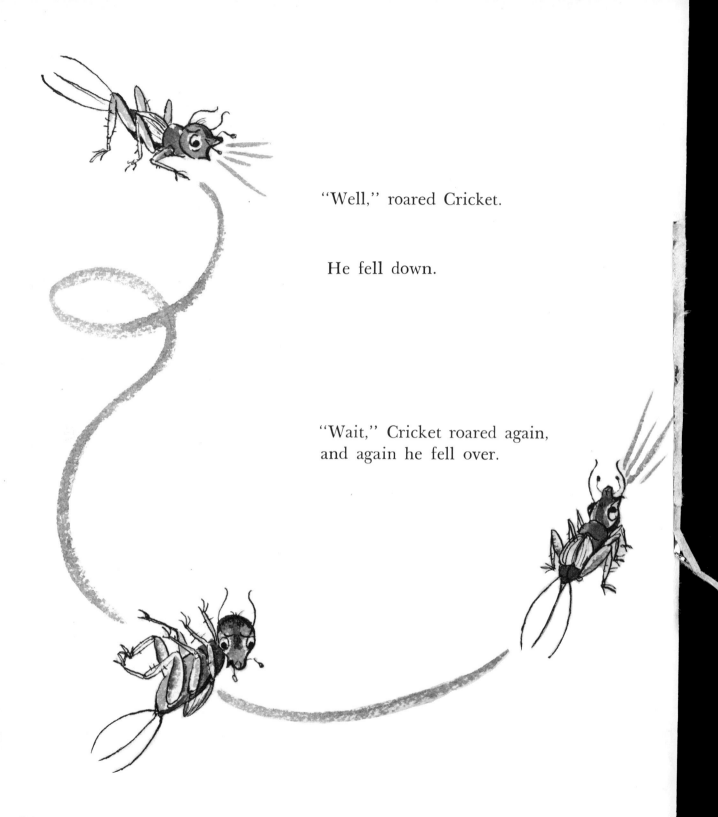

"Well," roared Cricket.

He fell down.

"Wait," Cricket roared again,
and again he fell over.

"What's the matter with this voice anyway?" he asked sadly. "It keeps knocking me over. It's bigger than I am."

"You're just not used to it," chirped Lion. He began to laugh. He laughed until the tears rolled down his face. "This silly little voice," he giggled.

"It tickles and tickles and tickles. Ha! Ha! Ha! Ho! Ho! Ho!" Lion rolled over and over in the grass, holding his stomach, just laughing and laughing and laughing.

Rooster opened his mouth to scold Lion for being so silly, and out came a long, low moo-oo-oo. Rooster looked around to see who was making that awful noise.

Pigeon growled and made a terrible face at Rooster.

Cat ran up a tree and crouched out on the end of a branch.

"Wait a minute," said Muffer. He was beginning to get a little worried about the way the animals were acting. "Cats don't fly."

"Well, this cat does," cawed Cat. She stood up on the very end of the branch and spread out her paws. "LOOK OUT, EVERYBODY! Here I come!" And down she came, tumbling end over end all the way. Luckily for her, she landed on the soft grass.

At that, Frog began to gobble nervously,
Pig began to buzz, and Duck barked and
barked and barked.

"Oh dear," said Muffer, looking around at the animals, at Cricket getting up and falling down; at Lion rolling in the grass and giggling; at Cat trying to fly; at Duck barking at Cow. "I think I had better go and get Mr. Hullabaloo."

"Please, sir, Mr. Hullabaloo," said Muffer, when he found the Sounds angel. "I'm afraid a few little things went wrong."

"Wrong? Nonsense!" Mr. Hullabaloo answered busily. "Just stick to the list. It's as clear as butter on bread."

"Yes, sir. Except, well, Donkey ate the list and . . ."

"*Bread and cheese and kisses!*" roared Mr. Hullabaloo when he heard what Muffer had done.

"This is a fine how-do-you-do," Mr. Hullabaloo said in a dreadful voice when he saw what the animals were up to.

"Here now," he called to Bear, who was picking daisies and cooing at a butterfly. "Back to the Sound Department at once! That means all of you," he said, waving his hands at the animals. "Each and every one of you."

"Well, I'm not getting up again," roared Cricket. "I'm black and blue all over from falling down."

"I'll carry you," Muffer said.

"It's a good thing," Mr. Hullabaloo gave Muffer a stern look, "that I have a copy of the list. First thing I want you to do, Muffer, is to collect their voices, and then .... *pitchers and ponies!* ... let's get this thing done right!"

"Yes, sir," said Muffer, very meekly.

"Cricket," called Mr. Hullabaloo. Cricket stepped forward. "Try this," said Mr. Hullabaloo kindly.

"Chirp. Chirp. Chirp." Cricket smiled. "Oh, this is fine," he sang. "Chirp. Chirp. Chirp," he said cheerily, and danced away. "What a happy *little* voice."

"Lion," called Mr. Hullabaloo. Lion stepped forward. "And you try this one," said Mr. Hullabaloo wisely.

Lion put his head back and roared. The animals shook with fright, and Muffer hid behind Mr. Hullabaloo quickly.

"Roar," said Lion. "Roar. Now that's what I call a voice. Roar," he said. "Out of my way," and he walked past with his head in the air, and a faraway look in his eye. He turned and looked at them all proudly. "I am the king," he said. "Roar."

One by one, Mr. Hullabaloo called up all the animals.

"Bear," said Mr. Hullabaloo, "it's your turn. Come and try your new voice."

"But I *like* the voice Muffer gave me," cooed Bear. "Why can't I keep it?"

"Because," said Mr. Hullabaloo very firmly, "crickets don't roar, and bears don't coo!"

"Not ever?" asked Bear sadly.

"Not ever!" Mr. Hullabaloo said.

"What *do* bears do?"

"Bears growl," said Muffer. "It says so, right here on the list."

"*Pigeons* coo," said Pigeon, showing Bear how it sounded.

"Growl," said Bear. He tried it again. "Grow-w-w-l." He looked very pleased. "Say," he said, "that's not bad for a beginner. I think I'll go into the w o o d s a n d practice. Growwll. Growwwlllllll."

"It came out right after all, didn't it, Mr. Hullabaloo, sir?" asked Muffer, very pleased. "And now that we're finished. . . ."

"Finished? FINISHED?" said Mr. Hullabaloo, in surprise. "Why, we've hardly begun. Just *look* at this list . . . sounds, sounds, sounds . . . hums and snaps and hisses and swishes, gurgles and ripples, hoots and wails and twitters and whines, echoes and trills . . . *dried apple pies!*" he cried. "Did you say FINISHED?"

"I guess not," said Muffer, sighing.

"Before we go on, however," said Mr. Hullabaloo, giving Muffer a stern look, "let's find out if we've learned something today."

"Oh, yes, sir," Muffer said quickly. "Yes, we have."

"And what have we learned?"

"We've learned," said Muffer, "that pigeons don't growl . . ."

"And?" asked Mr. Hullabaloo severely.

".... and bears don't coo!"